W9-CAI-730

Copyright © 2012

make believe ideas ltd
The Wilderness, Berkhamsted, Hertfordshire, HP4 2AZ, UK.
565 Royal Parkway, Nashville, TN 37214, USA.

All rights reserved. No part of this publication may be reproduced, stored in a retrieval system, or transmitted in any form or by any means, electronic, mechanical, photocopying, recording, or otherwise, without the prior written permission of the copyright owner.

www.makebelieveideas.com

Written by Tim Bugbird.
Illustrated by Lara Ede.
Designed by Annie Simpson and Sarah Vince.

Izzy the Ice-cream Fairy

Tim Bugbird · Lara Ede

make believe ideas

ice cream

Once upon a time,
in a **sunny**, sandy land,
lived **Izzy**, Mo, and Mia
at a pretty **ice-cream** stand.

The **fairy friends**
scooped ice cream
from their famous **ice-cream** well
to sell in **rainbow** flavors, in a crispy wafer shell.

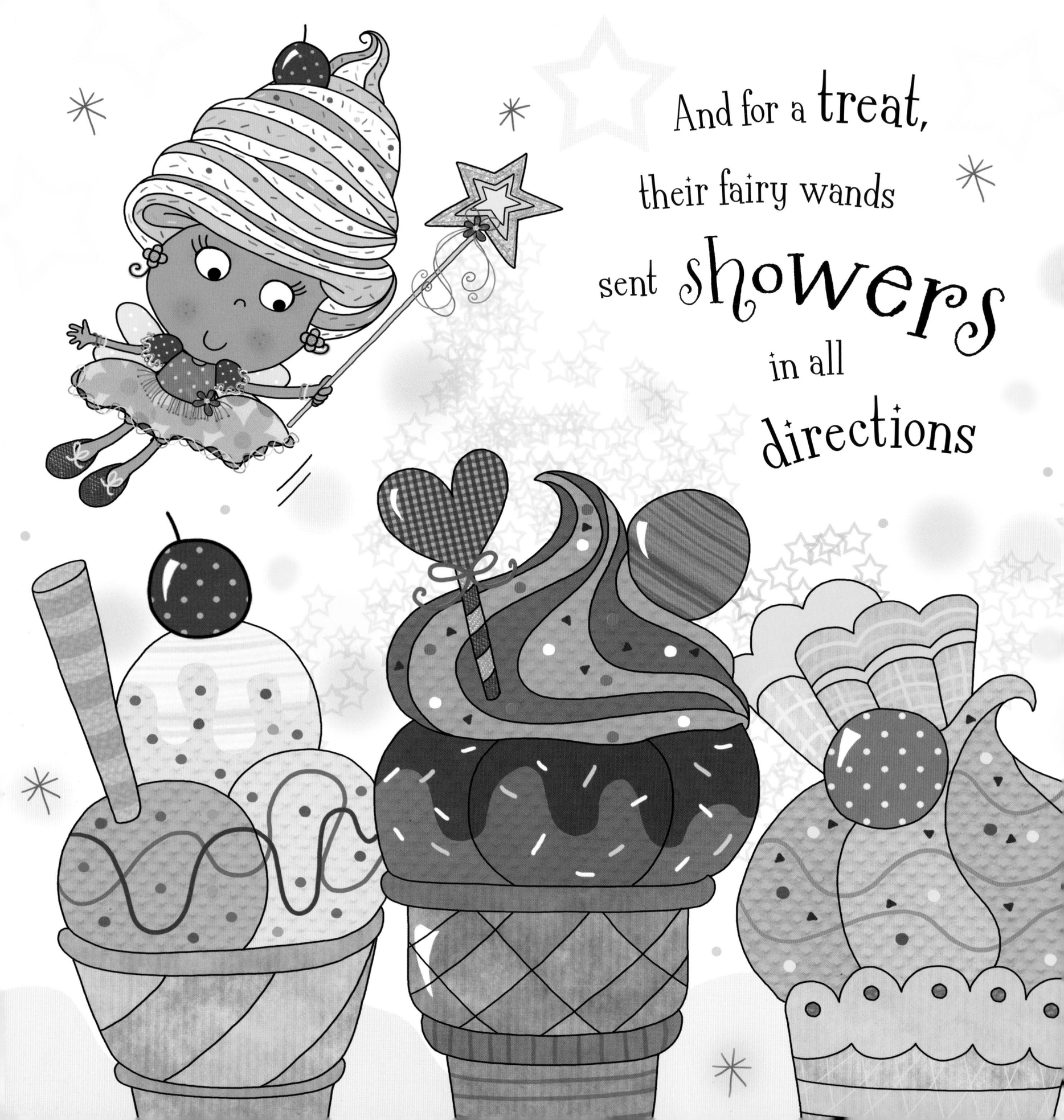

And for a treat,
their fairy wands
sent showers
in all
directions

of candy jewels
and chocolate chips,
to top the iced
confections.

They saved up every penny
to fund their carnival float

and every year, for Best in Show,
they won the fairies' vote!
1st

Then, early one summer,
they peered inside their well,
expecting flowing ice cream,
but there was nothing
left to sell!

The well had run
completely dry.
Why?
They had no clue.

But being modern fairies,
they knew just what to do!

Izzy surfed the fairynet for places cold and chilly
with ice cream in abundance, but the results were just
too silly!

If you said them fast enough,
they sounded almost right,
but two made Izzy laugh out loud,
and one was just a
fright!

"Where can I find **ice cream**?" Tap, tap, tap . . .

"No, that's not right!"

"No, that's not right!"

"No!

That's definitely

not right!"

Tap, tap, tap . . . ICE CREAM

Izzy finally found a place
with no palms, sea, or sand.
It was far away but perfect –
she'd discovered Ice-cream Land!

Without delay,
the friends took flight
to a place of ice-cream mountains,
with sprinkles falling from the sky
and fruit-filled,
syrup fountains!

"Welcome to our
magical land!" said
Her Majesty the Queen.

"It's such a
lovely place to live,
but there's just
too much
ice
cream!"

"You see, it covers everything, so things are getting lost.
I'm sure my bike is somewhere here,
buried in the frost!"

Izzy said, "That's funny,
our land is **warm** and **sunny**,
and since our ice-cream well ran dry,
we can't make any **money**."

"Can we work **together?** This feels like such good **luck**."
"Grab a **shovel**," said the Queen, "and I'll call

RENT-A-TRUCK!"

They dug and dug
and dug
and dug,
until it was quite clear,
their ice-cream haul
would be enough
to last at least a year!

The journey home
was hampered by fog
and long,
dark nights,

so Mo and Mia
lit their path
with lanterns and
fairy lights!

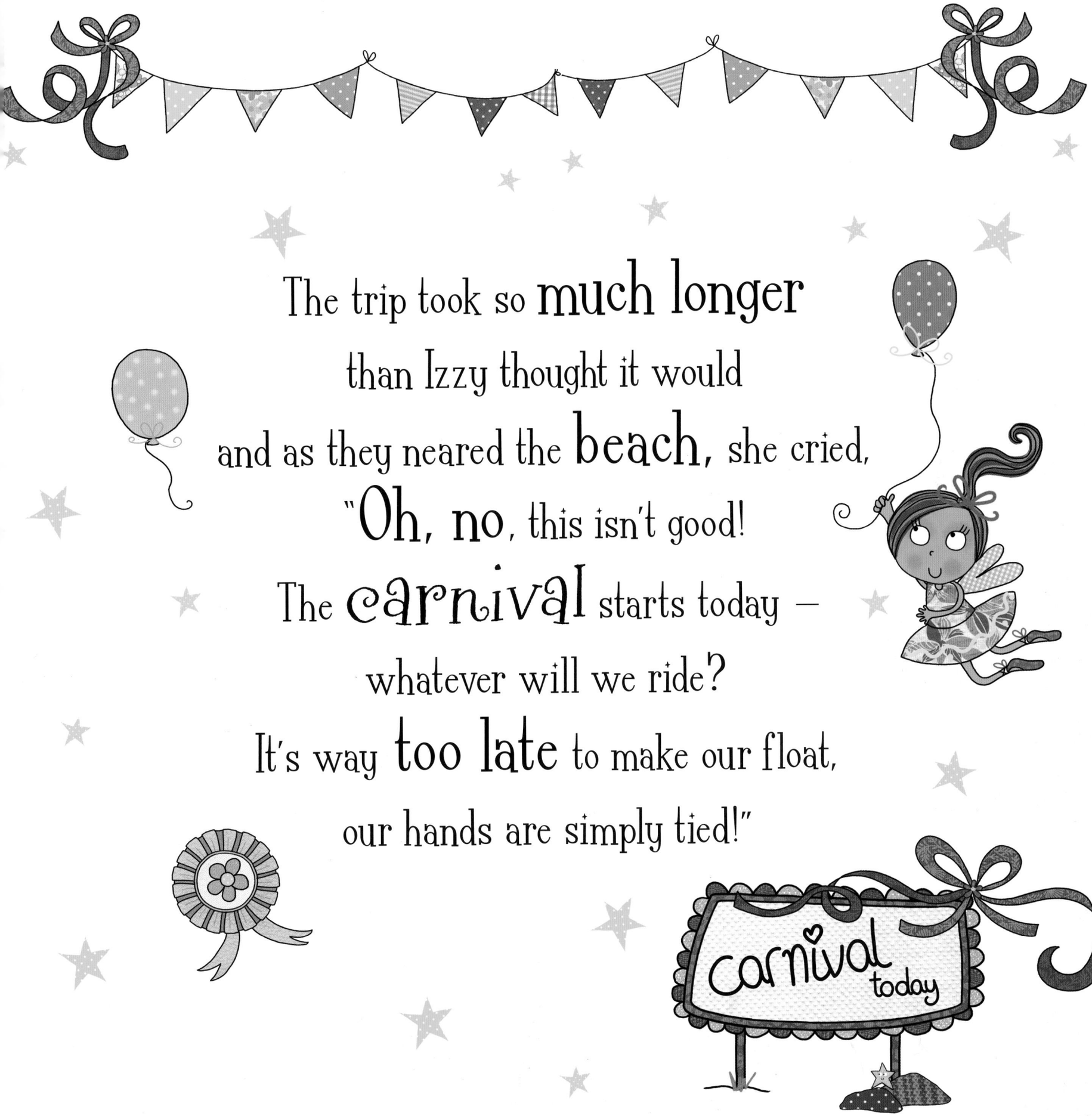

The trip took so **much longer**
than Izzy thought it would
and as they neared the **beach**, she cried,
"**Oh, no**, this isn't good!
The **carnival** starts today –
whatever will we ride?
It's way **too late** to make our float,
our hands are simply tied!"

But fortune had, for Izzy, one last **big surprise:**

all along the road ahead were floats of **every size!**

The fairies' truck joined the line, with its beautiful **glowing** lights.

It was just as good as a carnival float – a splendid, sparkling sight!

The fairies got to work,
serving ice cream to the crowd.
They made it home just in time
and had never felt so proud.

Their float did not win Best in Show,
but Izzy didn't mind,
for the love and joy that filled the day
was a prize of a better kind!

Izzy, Mo, and Mia made the perfect fairy team,
and now they knew just who to call when they needed more ice cream!